CLEAN SLATE

PIPER RAYNE

Cover design: Pink Ink Designs

Line Editor: Shawna Gavas, Behind The Writer

Chapter One

The office is quiet today. Then again, it's Monday morning and most people are either stuck in L.A. traffic, grabbing their lattes or just plain running late. Usually I enjoy the moment of solitude, but today things are different because when my boss, Jagger Kale, arrives this morning, I'm turning in my notice.

I pretend like I'm concentrating on my emails as I scroll through the short list I already answered last night. I jot down a to-do list of things I have to do before moving to Chicago and my gaze veers to the picture of Jade on my desk. The one personal item I brought after I felt secure enough to tell my boss I had a child. I shouldn't have worried so much. Jagger didn't care, as long as I did what I was supposed to and didn't call in sick all the time he was cool.

I smile and greet my co-workers who are staggering in with the Monday morning gloom on their face.

My cell phone dings and as I flip it around I secretly hope it's not Jagger telling me he's not coming in today. I'm not trying to be selfish, but I need to get this over with.

All weekend, I've tried to decipher whether he'll be mad or happy or indifferent to my departure.

The elevator door dings and I straighten my back, posed like the good employee in waiting. Another throng of co-workers empty out into the office but no Jagger. My eyes flick to the clock. It's not unheard of him to be an hour late, especially since Quinn reappeared in his life. My shoulders slump and I drink some of the Starbucks coffee I let myself enjoy this morning as a treat for making a big girl decision.

"Am I paying you to sip coffee?" Jagger strides by my desk, inserting the key into his office door.

His hair is damp at the ends, his suit as always wrinkle free. He bears no smile on his handsome face. All signs point to it being a normal morning except for his damp hair which means if I'm lucky, *he* got lucky this morning.

I stand, grabbing the extra cup of coffee off my desk and take out the plastic stopper before following him into his office.

"I grabbed you one on the way in."

He stands at the side of the desk, takes out his laptop, his eyes flickering to mine after he's completed the usual steps to his morning routine.

"Why do I deserve such royal treatment?" He looks at me skeptically.

What's that saying? You can't shit a bullshitter?

My hands press on the edge of his mahogany desk. "I get you coffee plenty."

A deep chuckle comes out of him. "Sure, when you told me about Jade, when you needed that week off to go to Chicago last month and the morning after you called in sick because you had a fever." He uses air quotes around the word fever to imply that I was lying.

"It was one hundred and four and people always get sick after they've been on planes," I argue.

The first smile I've seen this morning tilts his lips up. "Wouldn't know. I fly private."

I roll my eyes. Typical Jagger.

"So?" he asks, sitting down in his chair sipping the coffee I got him. He nods to the empty chair across from him. "What is it?"

I sit, my leg shaking, my foot tapping.

"Spit it out, Victoria." He raises both eyebrows.

He won't be so cocky once the words leave my mouth.

"I have to turn in my notice." My voice has never sounded so small and less like me. This job, with Jagger as my boss was on the con list of leaving, as much as I hate to admit it. Jagger isn't the easiest to work for, but I've grown used to our banter and underneath the façade he's actually a decent guy.

His entire body stills and somehow that's scarier to me than if he had popped up out of the chair in shock. He sets the coffee down in front of him on the desk, his forearms resting on the edge and his hands clasped together so tightly his knuckles are white. "What?" he says in a quiet voice.

I nod.

"I don't think I heard correctly," and coming from his lips it sounds more like a threat than a statement.

So, he's chosen the asshole approach. I shouldn't be surprised. His fiancé, Quinn, has made him a little nicer, but that snarky arrogant jerk is still alive and well.

"My mom...remember how I had to go to Chicago?"

He picks up his coffee again. "Yeah, the last time you brought me in coffee. That one was flavored. You should've gone the flavored route this time, too, if you were dumping this on my lap."

"Well—"

"And added a muffin."

"You don't eat pastries." I cross my arms in front of me.

"Right about now I want to sit in front of a plate of donuts."

I sink back in the chair. "My mom's sick, Jagger," I let the words spill out. I didn't want it to come to this. I wanted to give him the gist of my situation and leave.

"Sick?" He picks up his coffee, stands from his desk and heads to the couches. "Are you going to join me?" he asks.

I quickly stand and head over, sitting on the chair adjacent to him.

"I went to Chicago because they were running some tests. The diagnosis came in. She has MS."

"MS?" The wrinkles in his forehead tell me he doesn't understand the abbreviation.

"Multiple Sclerosis."

He nods in understanding. "I don't know much about it, but wouldn't the warm weather of Los Angeles make it better?" One side of his mouth ticks up.

Always the negotiator.

"Not when she has to leave her entire life, all she's ever known…her friends and family."

"You're her daughter. You should be the most important thing to her. Not to mention you should trump all others—you have the grandchild."

I purse my lips. "She won't leave, and I don't expect her too. Her entire life is still there."

"And your life is here." He crosses his leg, resting it on his ankle. "Surely, your ex has something to say about this."

I shrug.

"You haven't told the bastard yet?" He dips his head down to catch my eyes.

I shake my head. "Not yet."

"You're quitting your job before you tell your ex, knowing he could fight it and you might never leave L.A?"

"Oh, I'm leaving," I say with determination.

"Without Jade?" he asks.

My head shoots up and I lock gazes with him. "Never."

"So, next time you bring me coffee it'll be because you need help burying the body?" he asks, eyebrow quirked.

Jagger, Jagger, Jagger.

"Pete will understand." I wave that topic off. "That has nothing to do with this. I'm transferring the credits I have from school and applying to another school there. My mom needs me, and I have to go. It will be good for Jade to be closer to her grandma."

"I need you." He leans forward in his seat. "I'll double your salary."

I shake my head. "I can't stay."

"Hey, you loved Quinn's place, remember? She's selling it. I'll buy it for you and Jade."

I shake my head again, with a chuckle this time.

"Great neighborhood. I'm sure it probably has good schools, but can you really complain when it's free?"

"Jagger," I sigh. "I can't."

His shoulders sag and he leans back in his seat. "How long?"

"Two weeks?" I ask more for permission than anything.

"You expect to train your replacement in two weeks? It took me a year to mold you into the fine assistant you are today." He bites down on his lip to try to hide his smile.

"I'll make sure the transition will go smoothly."

"You better." He stands up, throws his coffee cup in the trash and sits down at his desk.

I follow waiting for instructions.

"What?" He looks up. "Go and do some work now." He shoos me away. "And I don't want some temp. Get me someone that's not going to leave me high and dry next month."

I nod, exiting his office and taking a deep breath before calling Human Resources to officially put in my resignation.

Jagger's right though, I need to tell Pete.

Chapter Two

I take a seat at the empty table in the restaurant Pete insisted we go to since we both love Mexican food. While I'm waiting for him I take in the décor and contemplate if we're even compatible in our food choices anymore. The white linen napkins and plush seating doesn't hold any resemblance to the street tacos we'd devour back in college.

"Tequila?" the waitress holds out the bottle for my viewing.

"Not tonight, thank you." I shake my head and she takes the shot glass away.

I pull my phone out, annoyed by Pete's tardiness. I guess in the past couple of years since we've been divorced, the part of me that was accustomed to his lateness shed like snake's skin.

I pull up Facebook and see that a few of my friends have posted some new pictures of their babies and their husbands—all smiling faces and adoring words.

"Crock of shit," I mutter, shutting down my phone before I hammer a post back about how many people lie on there. It's basically the highlight reel of anyone's life. And only the good parts. No one posts about how their spouse leaves his dirty socks laying around or how he eats chips in bed.

"You talking about this place?" Pete asks, sliding into the chair across from me.

His suit jacket is gone, the sleeves of his button down rolled up to his elbows.

"You didn't come from work?"

He takes the napkin, lays it on his lap and raises his hand to signal the waitress. "I did."

I remind myself that it's none of my business why he looks so relaxed.

"Oh."

The waitress comes over, holding the same bottle of tequila.

"Please," Pete says and then eyes me.

"None for me."

He nods and focuses his attention on the cute blonde ready to serve him. "She's in AA."

I don't even justify his lame joke with a response or an argument that I'm not. I also fail to mention I don't drink because *I'm* the one going home to our daughter tonight.

The waitress pours his tequila shot, he downs one and she pours another.

"What are we in college again?" I ask.

He downs the second one just for good measure, his eyes never leaving mine the entire time. He can stop with the 'you can't control me' act. I was never so grateful as to be fired from that job two years ago.

The waitress goes to pour a third, but he covers the glass with his hand.

"That's good, thanks."

"Turning into a light weight in your older years?" I smirk.

"Don't want us waking up in the morning together." He winks.

I pretend choke like I'm going to vomit. "Sober or drunk that's not going to happen. Go ahead and have a third." I cross my arms over my chest.

He removes his hand from the shot glass. "You heard the lady," he says to the waitress with a charming smile and she pours one more before walking away. I'm sure she's wondering why table seventeen is so weird.

He sips his drink this time, then places it down. "So, why have you summoned me here tonight? Jade and I stayed in last weekend and watched movies. I brought no women home and other than overdosing on pixie sticks, I was a good boy." His lips tick up in that playful smile that once drew me to him.

"She came home raving about the fort you made. You actually slept on the floor?" I pretend to peruse the menu, even though I figured out what I wanted half an hour ago since Pete can't tell time.

"In the middle of the night I snuck up onto the couch and before she woke up, I moved back down to the floor, but that's our secret. I made a pact with her."

"Go figure you not keeping good on a pact."

The playfulness drops from his face and his gaze holds mine. "Below the belt, Clarke."

I nod. He's right. "I'm sorry."

The cocky smile that gets him more pussy than I care to know about snaps back into place. "So?" he picks up his menu, glancing over it.

I twist the cloth napkin in my fingers. "Remember how I went to Chicago?"

He puts the menu down and focuses in on me. The

lawyer in him tipping him off that what I have to say is pertinent and it's almost ingrained in him to listen.

"Yes."

"My mom…the diagnosis came back, and she has Multiple Sclerosis."

He frowns. "I'm sorry."

Pete and my mom have never gotten along, but I know he understands what it took for me to move from Chicago to L.A. with him in the beginning of our marriage. And since he can still read me, I don't even have to broach the subject we're here to discuss.

"You want to move back?" he asks, his hand sliding across the table to his glass. He downs it and then raises his hand as the waitress is walking by. "Whiskey neat."

Once she leaves to fill his order, he starts playing with the fork, flipping and turning it over.

"I'm not sure what you want me to say." His voice has lost the boisterous tone it usually bears.

"I hate to ask, but with your hours…"

His palm goes up to stop me, which I do. "I know I can't keep her here. That week you were gone proved that. Until I find my next wife, which will be never, I can't have Jade full-time *and* have my career."

If someone other than me were sitting across from him, they'd probably think that was a horrible statement for a father to say, but truth is, Pete knows who he is, and he doesn't apologize for it. He's a workaholic defense attorney who works unhealthy hours. His only true time off is during the two weekends a month when he has Jade.

"I know it will be difficult, but I think it'll be good for Jade to be surrounded by the rest of her family. Besides this'll get you back in Chicago to see your parents more often and I'm sure they'll like that."

"Quit while you're ahead, Vic." He gives me a sad smile. "Have you found a job yet?"

I glance down at the table for a second. "Not yet."

"There's always McDonalds to fall back on."

"You know I can't cook." I break the somber mood quickly overtaking our table. "Or grill." I add, and we share a smile, both remembering our grill catching on fire on the patio of the house we shared when we were married. Needless to say, we never owned a grill again and Pete decided when people come over for dinner we cater.

The waitress sets the drink next to the shot glass. "Did you need a few minutes?"

"I think I lost my appetite." Pete hands her the menu.

"Come on. If you're going to drink that much." I eye his filled glass. "Then you're going to eat food. You brought me here, tell me what's good."

Okay, I admit it. I'm playing him. You don't go through a marriage like ours, one where you practically grew up together and not know what can turn a night around. Pete suggested this restaurant to show off. He loves to order for people, watch them eat something he was certain they'd like. I tell him I'm moving his daughter over two-thousand miles away and I'm letting him do what he loves. It's a win-win situation for both of us.

He studies me for a second and I'm double guessing my tactic before he finally speaks.

"We want all tacos." He smiles and then orders what's clearly more food than we'll consume.

"How long are we going to be here?" I ask once the waitress has left to tell the kitchen table seventeen will need barf bags included with their meals.

"Deal is if you want my daughter, you eat all the tacos." There's not one wrinkle of amusement on his face. Although, I've never really gotten the lawyer side of Pete the entire time I've known him, I can't help but think this is what he looks like when he's negotiating at work.

"Deal."

A smile cracks his composure and he shakes his head. "I always did hate your tenacity."

"I hate the way you turn everything into a negotiation." I smile back at him.

He nods understanding our own secret language. Usually I'd leave it at that, but the fact that he's allowing me to take Jade away says what kind of a man Pete really is and as much as I hate having to say the words, he deserves to hear them. "Thank you, Pete."

He nods again. "You just better make me up a room because we're going to have some sleepovers."

"Done."

Chapter Three

*T*he next day at the office, my stomach isn't sinking to depths I didn't know it had. I'm leisurely going through emails, flipping through some resumes that Heather from HR sent over that she kept on file. Not that I have the final say, but Jagger being Jagger has told Heather that everyone will be cleared by me before he sees them.

I swear, that man.

It's ten o'clock and Jagger hasn't called to tell me he's not coming in or going to be late. I have to remember that the schedule the man used to keep has been knocked off its axis by a pretty brunette.

The elevator dings and I wait to see who rounds the corner. There's my boss in his usual three-piece suit. I'm not going to lie, Jagger is a good-looking guy, but he reminds me way too much of Pete.

"Good morning." He inserts his key into the lock on his office door.

"You're being awfully polite." I stand to follow him in, our normal routine.

"I see you didn't bring me coffee." He eyes my hands as he pushes the door open and flicks on the lights.

"I don't have bad news today." I laugh, and his nostrils flare a little as he inhales.

Not at the joking stage yet. Got it.

"Lucky for you, the love of my life says I'm being an asshole. Oh, before I forget," he points at me, "You and Jade, my house in Malibu on Saturday. Quinn wants to have you over."

"Um."

He puts his hand up in the air, looking over the messages I had for him. "No excuses. Cancel whatever plans you have. We know the deal, what Quinn wants—"

"Quinn gets." I finish his sentence and he looks up.

"I knew you were a quick learner." He sits down at his desk, booting up his laptop. "You should be happy that's my motto because she also insisted I reach out to someone I know in Chicago." He nods at me to sit in the chair across from him.

"Reach out?"

"Have you found a job yet?" he asks, his forearms resting on his desk, his hands clasped together. The sunshine through the window glints off his silver wedding ring, which is still so strange to see.

"No." I clench my hands in my lap.

He shakes his head. "Victoria, Victoria, Victoria." He pretends to be reprimanding me. "Have I taught you nothing? Secure the job and *then* give your notice." His gaze flickers to my pad of paper. "You should jot that down for future reference."

My pen stays planted in my hand and I wait for whatever he's going to tell me.

"Before I tell you what Quinn suggested I do—I say suggested because I want you to remember *I* did it."

"Noted."

"I want you to say thank you, Jagger."

I stare blankly at him. "Let me know what it is and then I'll thank you."

The smile falls from his lips. "Disappointing. Maybe I should be happy you're leaving. I can have an assistant who will actually treat me with respect."

"Oh, we both know you don't want that."

He pretends to narrow his eyes and then faces his computer and starts typing.

"Remember Hannah Crowley?" he asks.

"The investor for Vance's film?"

Vance is Jagger's best friend whose script is being made into a movie.

"Yeah. Well, I had been talking with her a few months ago and she decided to start a foundation for…" He eyeballs the ceiling. "Women empowerment or for girls or something I don't fully remember. Anyway, guess what she needs?"

He asks me like he's the host of a game show.

"Who is an assistant?" I answer like I'm on Jeopardy, my tone thick with sarcasm. Though I can't deny the fact that he's found this out and might be able to get my foot in the door, is what makes him great.

"Ding, ding, ding. Give the woman a prize."

He spins the laptop around and on the screen is a woman on a couch holding a German Shepherd puppy while she stares down at some paperwork.

"I think you missed your calling in theater, Jag," she says, her smile warm and welcoming. I see the Skype symbol at the bottom of the screen.

"I'm good at everything, Hannah." He stands from his desk. "Now excuse me you two, my assistant forgot to bring me in a coffee this morning." He rounds his desk and I'm speechless. Number one because I wasn't expecting nor prepared to be interviewed by a potential employer today. Number two because I spilled an apple Danish on my blouse this morning and after spending ten minutes in the woman's washroom, I have a huge wet spot just over my breast.

Jagger closes the door behind him.

"Hi, Victoria. I'm Hannah." She waves like we're long-time pen pals who just got the opportunity to talk online.

"Hi. I'm sorry. I'm not prepared."

She smiles. "I know. No worries. I told Jagger I didn't want you prepared. I don't like all the nervousness and formalities of interviews, not to mention all the prepared answers. I'm kind of an odd duck." She shrugs while her hand keeps petting the dog who's now rolled up beside her on the sleek white couch.

"I'm just thankful for this opportunity. So, you're looking for an assistant?" I adjust the screen to try to hide the wet spot on my blouse.

"I am. I hate to say though, you'll be more of an office manager as well. We're starting small. Me, you and a marketing manager, but we'll have our hands in a lot of business."

"What is the foundation for?"

"RISE is the name and it stands for Respect, Inspire, Support, Empower. It's for young girls. My goal is to put programs in place for girls to meet and encourage one another to succeed. To find their own voice and use their own ideas to grow into well rounded women who are true to themselves. I'm probably going to go TMI on you now, but I come from a rich family and I didn't realize how ridiculous the values I was raised with were until I divorced recently and took a weed wacker to them. My mom taught me to marry well so I didn't have to work. I was expected to push my own dreams and aspirations aside to boost my husband's. Can you even believe it?"

She thumbs through her papers.

"This is our logo." She holds the piece of paper up to the screen.

"I love the whole thing."

I do, especially when I think of my own daughter, but I want to make sure this is secure.

"Great. So, Jagger didn't really give me a time frame for when you're moving here." She straightens her back, shifting in her seat and the dog stirs next to her.

Surely, I'm not hired?

"Three weeks. I gave my two weeks here and I need a week to pack everything up."

"You driving out?"

"No, we're flying. A moving van will be bringing everything a few days later." Thanks to Pete who volunteered to fly us first class because he didn't want me to drive Jade across country with no male to protect us. Insert eyeroll, I know.

"Great. That's perfect timing. One week to get situated in Chicago and then you can start in a month?"

"Hannah, don't you want to hear about my qualifications?"

She laughs and the dog jumps into her lap. "No. Jagger vouched for you and that's enough for me. I'm sure working for him is no picnic." She pushes the dog off her lap. "Lucy!" she scolds, but the dog keeps jumping, her nail snagging Hannah's sweater. "This thing cost me more than you did!" She screams watching the thread unravel as Lucy hops off the couch, the string still attached to her.

"Before I disrobe here in front of you, I better go. I'm sure my dog is going to relieve herself in my house if I don't let her out. Jagger mentioned that you have a daughter? I can't imagine if a dog is this hard to care for, how a human being must be?" She shakes her head and then all I see is her waist. "I'll get your number and email from Jagger, but welcome to RISE, Victoria." Her voice starts fading until all that's in the camera view is the white couch with Hannah having a stern conversation with her dog about etiquette and manners.

I shut the laptop lid and slide back into the leather office chair wondering if that was all a dream. Did he get me a job on his good word alone?

The door clicks open and he whistles on his way back to his desk.

"Done so soon?" he asks, sitting down in his chair across from me with a cup of coffee from the break room. "Why didn't you tell me about the break room situation?"

I crinkle my forehead.

"It stinks in there. People actually use the microwave?" You'd think someone just dropped a plate of pig's feet in front of him from the look on his face.

"Not everyone likes to eat out for lunch," I say.

"Did you know?" He leans forward. "People use actual mugs."

"Shame on them for caring about the environment."

"Anyway, how did it go?" he asks, changing the subject because he just mentally scratched off the break room from a place he'll visit again.

"She hired me," I mumble, still lost in a daze.

"Now will you say thank you, Jagger?" He leans back in his chair, his hands steepled with an arrogant smile in place.

"Thank you, Jagger," I say. "She hired me without knowing anything about me."

He shrugs. "I told her everything she needed to know."

"That's scary."

"Relax, Victoria. I know I give you a lot of shit, but you're a...good worker."

"Why?" I ask, standing up from the chair so I can continue my day.

"Why what?" He lifts the top of his laptop.

"Why did you do that for me? You're mad that I'm leaving."

He shakes his head. "I thought we got each other." He types in his password and then his gaze fixes back on me. "I'm selfish sure, but I understand why you're going back to Chicago. I probably wouldn't do it for my own mom given our relationship but look what I did for Marisol. I understand needing to be there for someone. But you have to promise not to tell anyone because I will deny it. You're a good person and I wanted to make your life a little easier."

I can't help the warm feeling invading my chest. "Is it too much if I give you a hug?"

He glances back at the computer screen, obviously uncomfortable with my appreciation. "Quinn is the jealous type. You wouldn't want to show up to work on your first day with a black eye, would you?" His gaze stays fixed on the screen in front of him.

"Again, thank you, Jagger. I'm not sure that's even enough."

"Hannah's going to be light on you. Don't slack on the job. I'll be checking in." Without ever looking away from his computer, he continues his day as I stare down at the man I once loathed as a boss.

Sometimes the most beautiful people come with a few sharp edges.

Chapter Four

"My girls!" my mom swings her front door open and holds out both of her hands.

Jade runs to her while trying to secure her backpack on.

"Don't worry, I got it all!" I yell ahead, but they're lost in each other's arms already.

I watch them embrace. My mom hasn't seen Jade nearly as much as she wanted to over the years.

Then I realize my legs are circled by suitcases.

"Thanks." I turn to the taxi driver and hand him the money.

"Jade come roll yours," I call, and she holds up her finger to my mom and runs back down the walkway.

"Everything's so dark here," she whispers when she reaches me. "Where's the sun?"

I chuckle, grabbing two suitcases. "You'll see it in May."

"But it's April next week."

"I'm kidding, Jade. It's dreary today that's all." I nod toward my mom. "Go to Grandma."

Jade walks up the path while I take in the neighborhood I grew up in. The street is the same. A few of the older multi-family homes on the block have been torn down and high priced single family homes with brick exteriors and black rod iron fences erected in their place.

"I know what you're going to say. And you're right. Pretentious, but they're good neighbors," my mom says as I reach her.

"They're nice," I comment. As I enter in one of the last Chicago bungalows on our block, I wonder how long before someone comes knocking on my mom's door to try and buy it out from under her.

"That they are."

"Are there any families? Kids for Jade to play with?"

She shoots me her you should know better look. "It's the city dear. No one is playing hopscotch on the sidewalks or riding their bike down to Irving Park."

I guess times are different than when I was a kid.

"I took that check you sent me down to St. Pat's Catholic School yesterday. Made sure to double check with the secretary and she's all set for Monday."

"Great. Thank you, Mom."

We walk into the house and instantly the smell of home wraps around me like a parka during a Chicago winter. Everything is the same as it was when I was here last, minus the snow thank goodness.

Jade throws her coat on the couch and runs down the hall. "Which bedroom is mine?" she screams.

"Your mom's old room," my mom calls down the hall.

I sit down on a chair in the living room, abandoning my own luggage by the front door.

"Do you want a drink or something to eat?" my mom asks.

"No, I just want to sit down for a second."

"You sat for six hours on the plane," she deadpans.

"Take a seven-year-old through two airports and tell me you aren't bone tired after you're done."

Thankfully, Jade is a very helpful and mature seven-year-old, but I kind of wish I would've taken Pete up on his offer to escort us to Chicago. But part of leaving Los Angeles was to have a clean slate and I couldn't do that with my ex footing the bill and helping me the entire way.

"She's an angel compared to you at that age." My mom tips her head and peers down at me.

"Why thanks, Mom." I'm surprised when she doesn't smack me on the back of the head over my sarcastic tone.

She sits down on the couch, her feet propped up on the coffee table. "When do you start?"

"I have to go in on Friday just to meet Hannah and the marketing manager and get acquainted. It will be quick and then I start on Monday."

"I'll take care of Jade. We have some catching up to do anyway. I can pick her up from school, too."

"Mom. I didn't move here so you could be Jade's babysitter."

"If you thought it was so you could be *my* babysitter, you're wrong. I'm fine. I can walk and talk and feed myself." There's joking in her tone, but an underlay of warning.

She's stubborn and what can I say? The apple fell right out of the tree with me. She's hard-working and not about to let anything slow her down. I'm here to make sure she doesn't overdo it.

"Walking three blocks to get her isn't going to be a big deal. Not to mention it'll be good for me."

I'm not going to argue with her right now. I'll wait until I can find a babysitter or maybe a mother who lives nearby to walk her home with her own child.

"Thanks, Mom," I say, which is the only thing that will appease her in this moment because I'm not starting the next world war within the first five minutes of being here.

"You're welcome. Glad that he let you come." She pats my leg, standing up.

By he, she means Pete. We never refer to him by name in the house.

"He's nice like that."

"Don't go letting him fool you. Now he can live the bachelor life all month long." She leaves the room before I can argue back.

All she sees in Pete is the man who hurt her little girl similar to the ways my dad hurt her. Talk about a sick and twisted cycle.

"Mommy. Mom!" Jade runs into the living room with my mom's cat Moe in her arms.

I inch back a little because he's not always pleasant.

"Look at Moe." She squeezes him so tight around the neck I fear his head is going to pop off. "Can he sleep with me?" she asks.

"Sure," I say. I'll let her know later that it's never going to happen.

Moe is like a night crawler, suddenly you wake up and he's wrapped around your neck. We'll be shutting our doors.

"Who wants pizza?" My mom comes in with a stack of pizza place menus. Gotta love Chicago, there's a pizza joint on every corner.

"Yay!" Jade starts jumping around the room with Moe hanging in her arms.

"How about Gino's?" I ask.

"The one off Lincoln? I'll call." My mom disappears to use her home phone in the kitchen.

Jade sits on my lap with Moe who looks nothing short

of unenthusiastic about his new house guests, especially the little one. "Mom?"

"Yeah?"

"Is daddy going to come visit?"

I couldn't tell Pete that he couldn't see us off at the airport—I'm not that cruel—but it did leave a crying girl in my arms until after take-off. I couldn't even bribe her with a Frappuccino from Starbucks.

"Yep and he promises to call."

She shoots me a look because although Pete is hands on while face-to-face, time slips past him when it comes to phone calls.

"We can video chat with him, too."

Her eyes light up. "He said he's going to get me a phone."

"We'll talk about it." I push the conversation away. She's seven and does not need a phone. I mentally tag that topic in my head to discuss with Pete.

"Pizza is on its way." My mom comes in and Moe squirms to get out of Jade's hold, meowing and jumping next to my mom.

Jade isn't easily detoured and follows him, petting him as he lays next to my mom. He decides to tolerate the unwanted attention.

"Thanks again, Mom."

"Stop thanking me. You girls are the ones who uprooted your life to move here."

"We're happy to do it." I smile.

"Yeah, we're happy to do it." Jade mimics me and smiles over at my mom.

"It's so great to have my girls with me. We're going to have so much fun." She squeezes Jade into her side.

I watch the two knowing that regardless of how hard

of a decision this was, it was the right one. I know Pete grabbed the short end of the straw on this one and I'll have to remember that the next time we disagree on something. Right now, after all the disappointing men in my life, I'm happy to be surrounded by the female race.

Chapter Five

 I stop outside the deli that Hannah told me was on the street level of our office building and take a deep breath, trying to shake the nerves away. After steeling myself for a moment, I open the door on the right to be greeted by a long hallway with elevators on the left-hand side.

"First day?" A woman's voice says as I take another deep breath and hesitantly press the up button.

I turn to my left to find a blonde in a blue dress and heels who looks like she just stepped off the cover of Vogue. Strike that, not Vogue, more like Cosmo. Yeah, Cosmo.

"Kind of." I hold my bag in front of me with both hands clasped to the handles.

"I'm Chelsea. I started working on the twenty-first floor with a non-profit a couple months ago. What floor do you work on?"

I smile. "Twenty-first."

She points. "The assistant?"

I nod.

She adjusts her bag up onto her shoulder and extends her arm out toward me. "Hi. I'm the marketing manager. Chelsea Walsh."

I shake her hand. "Victoria Clarke."

"Nice to meet you. Hannah hired me two months ago and we've been trying to do a lot of it ourselves, but I'm so happy you'll be joining us. I've been busier than a five-dollar hooker."

I smile, not sure what to make of her comment when the elevator dings open and we file in. She presses the button and we wait.

She checks out my hands. "No ring. Single?"

"Divorced."

She nods. "Me, too. Not the best club to be a member of, but more often than not, it's a happy club. Am I right?" She elbows me like we're a bunch of guys razzing each other about who will win the super bowl.

I smile.

"Isn't dating a let down? I went out with this guy recently because he had a motorcycle. Yeah, I love the bad boys. You'd think my ex would've ruined that for me. Sadly, still think I can change them." She waves off her last comments like they're nothing important. "So...this guy picks me up on his motorcycle and yeah, I know it's Chicago and cold but what am I going to say? Pick me up in your Honda? No way." She inhales a breath and I can see where she might be lightheaded with the way she's talking so much. "I thought we'd go along the lakefront or something, but he drives me to some upscale bar in the suburbs to hang around outside with his other wannabe bad boy biker gang, minus any *SOA* vibes."

"Bummer." I'm not sure what else to say. I've never met anyone as open as this woman is with a practical stranger.

"Bummer's right. It turns out the bike wasn't even his.

It was his dad's. Can you believe that? The kid—and I say kid because he lied about his age. He was twenty-one." She holds up her hand. "I'm all about dating a younger guy, but there's no way this kid who stole his daddy's bike was going to know his way around the erogenous zones. Am I right?"

"You're right." I look up to the elevator buttons. Thankfully, it lands on twenty-one and the doors open.

"I wanted to ask him for his daddy's number."

She laughs and we both step off the elevator into what is our new office.

Small is right, but it's quaint and cute. There's a small reception area for guests to wait with leather chairs and a couch. Magazines are fanned out on a coffee table with a cooler full of water bottles in the corner in case they're thirsty.

"What are you talking about?" The woman I've only seen through a video appears from down the hall. "Victoria!" she exclaims like I'm some long-lost sorority sister.

"Good morning, Ms. Crowley," I say, and she stops dead in her tracks. Her arms falling to her sides and her exuberant expression falling.

"No, no, no. Call me Hannah. You need to forget everything Jagger ever taught you." Her arms stretch and embrace me in a hug that I lightly reciprocate with a few pats on the back. She pulls away probably sensing my timidness. "Welcome." A soft smile crosses her face. "What are you carrying on about?" she directs her question to Chelsea.

"Well, it's Monday," she singsongs, her head bobbing back and forth.

"Oh yes, divorcee dating recap?" Hannah rolls her eyes in a cute, playful manner to say she secretly enjoys them.

"You guessed right."

"You'll have to fill me in in a bit." Hannah says, leading me over to a desk situated near a window. "Here's your desk."

My desk is gray and has a large screen monitor on it, a holder full of pens, notebooks and a phone. Everything looks all set for me to start.

"Looks great. Thank you so much."

Chelsea smiles on from across the desk. "Hannah, did you know she's divorced, too?"

Hannah nods "And she's got a daughter. Jade, right?"

"Yeah." I take out the picture frame from my bag and place it on my desk. Whether or not I get fired, this time I'm not ashamed to be a single mom. I should be proud to raise a daughter and not thinking my boss will perceive me as someone who will constantly be calling in sick.

"She's adorable." Chelsea wastes no time to pick up the frame and inspect it. "She looks just like you."

Poor Pete. We both hear that all the time. But I see a lot of him in her, especially in her character.

"We're like the modern-day version of the First Wives Club." Chelsea places the picture back down. Both Hannah and I look over at her, not understanding. "You know, that movie with Diane Keaton, Goldie Hawn and…" she snaps her fingers. "What's the other one's name?"

"Bette Midler." I chime in.

She places her hand up in the air. "Are you a movie lover, too?"

"Oh, that one where they seek revenge on their ex's?" Hannah asks.

"That's the one. We're kind of like them except we're not going to extort our ex's," Chelsea says. "Though I would've if mine had had anything worth having."

"Mine is probably dating someone half his age," Hannah says with disgust in her voice.

"Mine is probably in jail right about now," Chelsea adds.

"Mine is a workaholic." My story doesn't sound nearly as bad as these two. "But I do have to have constant communication with him because we share a child."

They both laugh.

"True." Chelsea says. "I thank the heavens I didn't end up knocked up with my bastard of an ex. No offense."

"None taken." I look down at the picture of Jade, knowing Pete in my life isn't half as bad as having Jade not in it.

"Hold on girls." Hannah walks down the hall.

"There's a small break room down there," Chelsea says.

Hannah returns a minute later with a bottle of champagne and three coffee to-go cups.

"We're going to celebrate. To the kick off RISE. To us starting our lives over. To being free of controlling males."

She pries the bottle open easier than I could've and pours us each a drink. Placing the bottle down, she holds up her cup. "To a clean slate and new adventures."

Chelsea and I knock our paper cups against hers. "To a clean slate and new adventures," we say in unison.

As the bubbles from the champagne tickle my throat, I smile, knowing I made a good decision coming here. Surrounding myself with a duo of empowering women, helping my mom and raising my daughter without a man in my life sounds like the perfect way to start over.

Looking back, that sentiment seems laughable given what happened the following week.

THE END

Can Victoria start over when she runs in
to the BEST MAN from her wedding
at morning drop-off?

**Come to our table to grab your exclusive CODE
for a FREE copy of MANIC MONDAY!**

Chapter One of Manic Monday

MY HAND SLAMS down on my alarm, but instead of shutting the bloody thing off, the screaming banshee slides off my nightstand and drops to the floor. I peek out one eye and the immediate sight of the clutter of clothing and boxes in the makeshift bedroom makes me want to squeeze it shut again. The piercing sound of my alarm still rattles inside my head as its cacophony continues from the floor. My palm continually slaps the wood, hoping to make contact with the cord so that I can yank the damn thing up and shut it off.

"Mom?" my daughter Jade calls out to me.

I swivel my head in the direction of her voice and there she stands in her poop emoji pajamas with my alarm poised in her hands like she's offering me a gift.

"Turn it off," I groan and bring the pillow over my head.

Her small feet pad along the hardwood floors, squeaking right at the edge of my bed. The pillow gets plucked from my grasp, and seconds later the overhead light flickers on, blinding me temporarily.

"You're going to be late." My mom's voice adds to the mix from down the hall.

I dream of being woken up by some suave foreign man

who doesn't speak a lick of English, while he uses his soft, roaming hands and sprinkles kisses over my flesh to stir me into consciousness. Instead, I get my seven-year-old daughter and my mom to orchestrate my Monday morning trip to Crazyville.

Jade turns off the alarm and sets it down on the nightstand. "It's seven," she says in a completely unalarmed tone.

"What?" I sit up, chip crumbs falling to the rumpled sheets.

"Eating in bed again?" She giggles, and I snatch her up by her waist pulling her onto the bed with me, using my fingers as an instrument to torture her. Torture by tickle.

"Mom, no!" She laughs and squirms.

"It's only six-fifteen."

She wiggles enough to slide away and I release her because I'm later than I usually am, but it's Monday and since I made a deal with Jade that every Sunday is our day, it meant a late night of studying after she went to bed.

"I'll turn on the shower." She walks out of the room and straight into the small bathroom of our three-bedroom bungalow—the house I grew up in. Jade now sleeps in my old bedroom, while I'm shacked up in my mom's old sewing room. She doesn't sew much these days, anyway.

"Thanks, and then—"

"I know. Brush my teeth, get dressed, and comb my hair."

I smile at my independent daughter even though it causes a familiar tug on my heart. She should have had the luxury of having a mom who picks out her clothes and does fancy hairstyles with ribbon and curls before school. A mom who wakes *her* up with the smell of bacon and pancakes and freshly squeezed orange juice. A dad who pulls her mom in close to say goodbye and promises to be at her soccer practice as he kisses the top of her head.

Instead, she's got a dad who didn't blink when I told him we were moving back to Chicago and leaving him in Los Angeles. A mom who gave up her own education only to pursue her degree later in life while she's working a full-time job. A mom who moved her halfway across the country, leaving behind the beach and sunny weather for concrete and dreary rain-filled days.

To her credit, my tough girl never gave me a guilt trip when I sat her down and explained that Grandma needed us. She packed her boxes and hid the tears. I guess people are right when they say she's the spitting image of me.

I get up from the bed, staring at my phone to make sure my new boss, Hannah, hasn't sent me anything urgent. It's not something she expects me to do. But it's been a hard transition from my last boss, Jagger Kale, who expected an answer to any question whenever he asked it. Old habits die hard.

Setting it down, I grab my robe and head out of the cocoon of soft sheets, warm blankets, and quiet space to start my week.

Forty-five minutes later, my heels click on my mom's linoleum kitchen floor.

My to-go cup of coffee is placed next to my purse and my computer bag, while Jade is shoveling Lucky Charms into her mouth, leaving her banana untouched. My mom is still in her pajamas reading the paper mindlessly nodding and agreeing with Jade on the latest second-grade drama at her new school.

"Then Brian told Peter that he liked Valerie and—"

"Whoa," I stop her, sliding my arms into my jacket. "Like? You're talking about friendship, right?"

Jade rolls her eyes and I glance over my shoulder because surely, she's not rolling her eyes at me.

"Mom," she sighs.

My mom curls the corner of the newspaper to eye me over her reading glasses.

"You shouldn't be liking any boys."

"I don't." Jade notices me getting ready, stands, takes her bowl to the sink and grabs her jacket.

I hold out her backpack for her and she slides her arms through it.

"Good because—"

"Boys only detour you from obtaining your dreams. Make your own path for yourself before you allow others to walk beside you," she says in a deadpan voice beyond her years.

"Sorry." I bend down and kiss her cheek. "It's the truth though," I whisper.

Again, the paper peels back, my mom's face showing her displeasure over what I'm teaching her granddaughter.

Jade wraps her arms around my mom's neck, pressing her lips to her cheek. "Love you, Grandma."

My mom pats her arm. "Love you, bug, I'll be outside at school's end." Then she lowers her voice and whispers. I could probably dictate her secret conversation with Jade. She's telling her to open her heart and see the possibilities this wonderful life has to offer.

It's a crock of shit that I used to believe, and it landed me right where I am.

"Thanks, Mom. You sure you're good to meet Jade after school because—"

"I'm good." Her eyes sternly warn me to let the topic go.

My mom might be a softy when it comes to love, but she doesn't allow others to question her ability.

Following Jade's lead, I bend down and kiss my mom's cheek. "Love you. Call me if you need me."

"Uh-huh." She continues to read the paper. "Have a good day."

We grab our stuff and head out the door, so I can walk Jade the three blocks to school. We don't finish walking one block before Jade asks a question that has me wanting to come to an abrupt stop if I weren't already so late.

"What kind of dad is Daddy?"

"Kind?"

Jade jumps from sidewalk square to sidewalk square. "Yeah, like he used to be Weekend Dad because I only saw him on the weekend."

"Where did you hear that expression?" Damn Google. My seven-year-old daughter thinks she's seventeen.

She shakes her head adamantly. "Nowhere."

I shoot her a look with my chin down, eyes wide. Basically, the stern mother look.

"Promise." She holds out her pinky. "Swear."

I pinky swear with her. Knowing my daughter would have crumpled like a cheap suit if she was lying.

"Your dad is just your dad. He'll come and visit, maybe we'll go back and visit him from time-to-time. He might not be able to come every weekend, but that's what's so great about technology."

I say this even though the dipshit has only Skyped with her four times in the past two months. Whatever, I'm being the bigger person here.

"Yeah, but at school, Valerie says her dad is the Date Night Dad. Every Wednesday he picks her up from school and they go to dinner and a movie. He always has a present for her."

"That's nice." My heart clenches over the fact that she

35

doesn't, and likely never will, have that type of relationship with her father.

She says nothing.

I knew this move would be hard on her. Miles away from a dad who never really put her first to begin with, his eye set on making partner at his firm and nothing else.

"Maybe my dad is a Sometime Dad?"

The line of cars on the road ready to drop off their children signals we're nearing the school. The giggles of children mix with the hollering of mom's I love yous. Teachers are ushering kids in through the front doors when we approach, but I stop Jade and bend down to her level.

"Jade," I say, squeezing her shoulder. "Your daddy misses you and I know sometimes he works too much to call, but always know, he's thinking of you. You're his little girl."

She nods. "I get it. He wants to be successful and make a lot of money because Nana and Papa didn't have a lot."

I ignore the spark of anger inside me. Pete needs to watch what he tells her. Money is not everything in life. No one gives a shit what your bank account balance is when you die.

"He just wants to make sure you have everything you want." I tuck a strand of her brown hair behind her ear.

I don't add in that he also wants a new sports car for himself, the condo on the beach, and all the other material things that attract the women whose biggest goal is to score a rich husband.

"He said he sent me a present." Her eyes light up and I really hope she receives it this time around.

"See, he's always thinking of you." I open my arms and she rushes in squeezing my neck.

"Love you, bug," I whisper in her ear.

"Love you, Mommy."

We part ways and she skips ahead of me. "So, Some-time Daddy then?" she asks.

Should've known I couldn't deter her from defining her daddy's role in her life. She's persistent.

"I'd prefer just Daddy, but..."

"Yeah, I'll tell the kids I have a Sometime Daddy."

We reach the steps of St. Patrick Catholic School, the buzz of early morning in full force. Two familiar moms stand at the bottom of the staircase sipping their coffees and having their usual morning chat about every other parent's incompetence in the school.

"Victoria," Darcie coos, pushing her long blonde hair over her shoulder. "Jade," she says my daughter's name like she's been bouncing on the balls of her feet all morning to see her.

"Darcie. Georgia." I bend down and tighten Jade's ponytail, smoothing out the wispy unruly hairs. "Have a great day. Grandma will be here after school."

"Okay. Love you, Mommy." She gives me a looser hug than she did moments ago and before I'm standing upright again, she's with a red-haired girl talking nonstop as the two venture up the stairs.

"Have a great day, ladies." I turn to leave and head to the train station.

"Oh, Vikki," Darcie says. I knew it would be asking too much to sneak away.

I smack on my court smile. The smile I had perma-nently fixed on my face when my ex and I were going through the divorce. The Stepford creepy-wife one that says I'm content and even-keeled, when really, it's like World War Z in my head.

"Victoria," I clarify for the five-hundredth time since we moved here.

"As you know, the carnival is a month away and since

you missed the parent meeting, we signed you up to run an event."

I stare blankly at her. Mostly because I will lose my shit and that will not help Jade with this transition. We need St. Pats. It's the closest school to my house and it's a good one.

"What event would that be?" I ask with the patience I can only assume I honed well while I was working for my old boss, Jagger Kale.

When exactly is this carnival? I don't even know if I'm available. And a carnival? Seriously, get a new idea. It's not the eighties.

"Your choice," queen bee says. "Just make sure there's no food involved. All food has to be inspected before coming in. We don't want anything that could endanger the children. That should be easy for you, right?"

Again, I stare blankly at her, trying to compose myself before I grab her Starbucks cup and squeeze it until it soaks her ridiculous khaki belted jacket.

Hello, if I was a stay-at-home-mom and had all this time on my hands, I'd be sporting the 'I'm on my way to the gym outfit' when in reality I'm going home to lay on my couch And the only reason I'd be wearing yoga pants is because they won't impede the pound of chocolate I'm going to consume. Ladies shouldn't be ashamed of the bonbon stereotype. Everyone knows a mom's real work is from six to eight in the morning and three to nine at night.

"Great, I'll arrange something," I say with a smile and a nod, then turn to step away before I tell her what I really think of her signing me up for something without my consent.

Like a flash of lightning in the sky, the sight of the smiling man leading a little boy up toward the school stuns me. I stop and stare, my mind blank.

I don't think about the Sometime Daddy dilemma, or

getting to work on time, or the carnival event I have to plan. Instead, I try to figure out how many years it's been since I last saw Reed Warner.

Come to our table to grab your exclusive code for a FREE copy of MANIC MONDAY!

About the Author

Piper Rayne, or Piper and Rayne, whichever you prefer because we're not one author, we're two. Yep, you get two USA Today Bestselling authors for the price of one. Our goal is to bring you romance stories that have "Heart-warming Humor With a Side of Sizzle" (okay...you caught us, that's our tagline). A little about us... We both have kindle's full of one-clickable books. We're both married to husbands who drive us to drink. We're both chauffeurs to our kids. Most of all, we love hot heroes and quirky heroines that make us laugh, and we hope you do, too.

Goodreads
Facebook
Instagram
Pinterest
Bookbub
www.piperrayne.com

Join our newsletter and get 2 FREE BOOKS!
http://bit.ly/2tsNcpP

Be one of our UNICORNS and join our Facebook group!

Also by Piper Rayne

The Modern Love World

Charmed by the Bartender

Hooked by the Boxer

Mad about the Banker

The Single Dad's Club

Real Deal

Dirty Talker

Sexy Beast

Dirty Truth

The Manny

Doggie Style

Chore Play

Bedroom Games

Cold as Ice

On Thin Ice

Break the Ice

Charity Case

Manic Monday

Afternoon Delight

Happy Hour

Blue Collar Brother

Flirting with Fire

Crushing on the Cop

Engaged to the EMT